SOMEWHERE OVER THE RAINBOW

(Memoirs of a Wartime Evacuee)

Kenneth Wesley

WESLEY
SAXMUNDHAM SUFFOLK

First published in Great Britain, 2009

British Library Cataloguing-in-Publication Data.
A catalogue record for this book is available from the British Library.

Arthur H. Stockwell Ltd bears no responsibility for the accuracy of events recorded in this book.

ISBN 978-0-9561980-0-6
Printed in Great Britain by
Arthur H. Stockwell Ltd
Torrs Park Ilfracombe
Devon

SOMEWHERE OVER THE RAINBOW
(Memoirs of a Wartime Evacuee)

This short account has been published to mark the seventieth anniversary of the outbreak of the Second World War in 1939. Part of the proceeds from the sale of this book will be used to help support the ongoing work of the Royal British Legion.

There is a word . . ., a rare, and oft' forgotten, or misused word, which in itself is more to my heart, – than any other . . ., that WORD . . ., is - -
'ENGLAND'.

Sir Winston Churchill.

DEDICATION

To Mum and Dad, Nan and Granddad (White), Norman and Ron, and also to my dear wife, Brenda, who has listened patiently to the recounting of these events quite a few times in the past.

CONTENTS

THE OUTBREAK OF THE SECOND WORLD WAR

When I look back now upon that awful event, the outbreak of the Second World War at the beginning of September 1939, I find myself wondering what thoughts were in the minds of my parents - and, indeed, what pressures and anxieties may have been put upon them by the media and the government - when they allowed my two brothers and myself to be evacuated. We were taken from our home in East London to Suffolk, as part of the first evacuation scheme to be 'tried out'! We were only seven, eight and nine years of age at the time. I was the middle one, but although I was only eight years old I still have some vivid recollections of that dramatic historical event.

The clouds of war had been gathering and growing ominously, month by month, since at least the beginning of the year, and we had all been called upon to take part in the new experience of queuing up for things! First of all, there were the long silent queues at a nearby school for identity-card registration. My number was TXDO 167 5 - whatever that may have meant to someone! Well, at least *I've* always remembered it!

Then there were the queues for the issue of gas masks, coupled with the unpleasant business of trying the things on. Three types of gas mask, I believe, were issued. The smallest was a sort of enclosed grey rubber basket, with a front visor and a side pump, for very young babies. The next-sized one was called a 'Donald Duck'. It was in red and blue rubber with two round eye pieces and a rather funny nose attachment. It was for children up to, say, the age of six. The rest of us were fitted out with the standard-issue gas mask, in various sizes. This had a front visor and round filter piece below it, and black rubber straps that were pulled very tightly back over the head to hold it firmly in position.

It was during this 'fitting and issuing' process that some of the old Cockney humour and spirit began to emerge. Sober-faced parents tried to make light of the whole affair in front of their children. Many of us stood wrestling with the new contraptions, pulling faces and laughing at the weird sight of one another; and some of the men made loud noises, expressive of exasperation and frustration, to raise a few more laughs for the benefit of the youngsters present. Even so, some of the younger children had screaming fits, and their mothers had bouts of mild hysteria at the prospect of what this might all mean in the end. The situation might have got out of hand were it not for the officials who presided over the whole affair in a most calming and efficient manner.

In my experience, the gas mask was an awful thing to wear. We did have to practise wearing them at the beginning of the war, but a gas mask was not an item that one could ever get used to. Thank goodness we never had to wear them for the real thing!

To crown it all, we had to queue up again a few weeks later, to have another green metal filter taped on to the end of the existing one. Apparently there was something else that we needed to be protected against.

There must have been quite a bit of paperwork and organisation done by the authorities to get the members of the public as far as the gas-mask stage, but there was even more to come. Within a few weeks, a questionnaire arrived for each household to specify its needs in respect of an air-raid shelter. The shelters were of two types: the indoor Morrison shelter was basically a steel-framed cage, designed to fit under a dining-room table; and the outdoor Anderson shelter which was comprised of corrugated-iron sheets, bolted together to form a shed-like structure, which was then half submerged in a large hole in the ground and covered with soil. These precautions, I assume, were carried out in all of the larger towns and cities at first, and then throughout the whole of the country, as the government gradually prepared the general public for another war.

A great many people still had the most horrifying memories of the First World War, which had occurred some twenty years or so earlier. They were appalled by the thought of a bloody conflict like the previous one. Therefore, the leaders of the government and the opposition pursued their policies of appeasement and negotiations with Adolf Hitler and the Nazi hierarchy. Throughout the summer months, efforts were made to try to find a peaceful solution to the demands that were being made by the Germans - but it was all in vain. The tone of the radio newsreaders' voices grew increasingly severe each day, as they broadcast news of the events which were gradually unfolding in Europe. The newspaper boys had a field day every day. Grim headlines were 'shouted' from the billboards every hour. As a result, the general public were being mentally tossed about, as though upon a stormy sea of hope and despair, during this time of great uncertainty and anxiety.

I have found myself backtracking, as it were, over those events which occurred before the evacuation finally took place at the beginning of September 1939. I hope that this additional information will have helped to set the scene for those decisions which then had to be made by parents. Looking back, after nearly seventy years, I feel it is important to highlight the real concern and anxiety people had with regards to the prospect of air raids and gas attacks being launched against this country.

My brothers and I attended Park School, which was opposite West Ham Park in Ham Park Road (all very aptly named!). The school was about ten minutes' walk from our little terrace house in Faringford Road, through the narrow alleyways and streets. I seem to recall that Mum and Dad, along with all the other parents, attended meetings at the school, at which plans for the evacuation scheme were outlined and discussed in some detail. They were also given a list of basic items of equipment, including clothing, shoes and toiletries, that every child would need to take with them in the event of the scheme actually taking place. Of course, the equipment also included the ubiquitous gas mask, which, shortly afterwards, would have to be carried by everyone almost everywhere.

At that time it was still a matter of personal choice for the parents whether their children left home or not, and many of them said no to the idea from the start. For them, that was the end of the matter - at least, for the time being. Others thought that, in view of the way in which the crisis was developing, the evacuation scheme might prove to be the best thing in the circumstances, and they went along with it. Once the parents had given their consent, however, that was it. They were on the list, as far as the school authorities were concerned, and contact was duly maintained with these families throughout the summer holiday period.

I can remember one afternoon of panic, when we were summoned to attend the school with our assemblage of basic items. My mother had to race round to the draper's store in nearby Vicarage Lane to buy me a pair of black plimsolls for one shilling and eleven pence three farthings (equivalent to about ten pence in present-day coinage), to complete my collection. When we arrived at the school - in a highly anxious condition, I might add - it turned out to be merely a practice run, to assess our state of readiness for the real thing. We were all checked out, given a bit of a pep talk about 'next time' by the teaching staff, and then allowed to return home (with a sense of such relief!) for a few more weeks.

I can remember playing cricket in the park with school friends, and lying in the grass afterwards, in the cool shadow of the tall plane trees, talking things over. The Territorial Army Headquarters were next door to the park, on the southern side, and the part-time soldiers were quietly going about their own preparations in a rather more sinister sort of way, we thought.

When the really hot summer weather finally arrived, people were soon talking about it being so hot that you could fry an egg on the pavement. I would not have fancied eating it afterwards. At the time, many of the men (older men, particularly) used to do a lot of spitting, perhaps as a result of having spent a lifetime in harsh working conditions, or as a result of smoking; I don't really know, but I do know that quite a lot of it used to finish up on the pavements. This might explain why some of the older women used to observe the early morning ritual, on those very hot days, of sweeping the tiny patch of pavement in front of their houses, and then scrubbing with buckets of water and long-handled brooms. On the completion of this task they would toddle off in their carpet slippers and hair curlers to the local off-licence for a jug of ale or beer, which they would then carry back home again hidden under their aprons.

In the afternoons, the ice-cream (Eldorado?) man would come, slowly pedalling his three-wheeled bicycle, with its dark-blue ice box mounted between the two front wheels. He would cycle around the narrow, dusty streets in the blazing heat, calling out, "ICES! Sur-luvly!" But people's minds were preoccupied with other matters, so he didn't get very many customers whenever he paused for a bit of a breather.

By this time, every passing day seemed to confirm the thoughts which were in everyone's minds: that our country was now heading, inevitably, towards war with Nazi Germany, and that life was about to change dramatically for each one of us. And change it most certainly did!

The negotiations with Adolf Hitler reached a crucial make-or-break point at the end of August, and finally broke down once again; so it was decided that the evacuation scheme should go ahead. I am not sure now whether we knew that this time it was the real thing, or whether, in order to placate us, our parents merely told us that we were going away for a few days. They probably left us with the thought that we would all be together again when the situation abroad improved. I remember that Dad came home from work on the Thursday evening and took my brothers and I around to the greengrocer's shop in West Ham Lane, where he bought us each a large peach (a very special treat at the time) to eat during the train journey the next day.

As we returned home, the paper boys on the street corners were yelling out the news of the evacuation. Pointing to the headlines on the billboards, Dad said, "Look! You're in the news! You're all famous!" His remark filled me with feelings of both mild elation and grey foreboding. We really were going this time, and nothing, it seemed now, could alter that fact.

The next day, the fathers and grandfathers had already left for work by the time we had assembled at the school, but the mothers and grandmothers (and even a few neighbours) were all there to see us off. There were a number of charabancs (that is, the older type of coach) lined up alongside the railings, outside the school playground area; and the teachers, with their white armbands, clipboards and whistles, were everywhere, trying to keep the rather emotional scene under some sort of control.

I think that children generally, in those days, were more respectful of parent and teacher authority. They knew that they had to do as they were told, especially when in their school environment. Nevertheless, there was a real outburst of drama and distress as the final words of goodbye were being said, and I seem to recall that a few copper coins (pennies and halfpennies) changed hands as part of the last-minute inducements. They came with the words "Here you are! You're a big boy now, so here's some extra pocket money to spend on whatever you like." The money came from parents and grandparents, and sometimes from absent relations, such as aunts and uncles. The thought of suddenly being considered grown-up, the extra money, and also the good wishes of unseen relations, made the departure even more of a sad experience for me.

We boarded the coaches and sat in the seats that our teachers directed us to. There were a few more tearful words, exchanged with some difficulty through the sealed windows of the coach, and a final roll-call was made before the driver started up the engine.

There was a chorus of loud cheering as, upon a given signal, we rumbled slowly off down the tree-lined road, away from Park School. Mothers and grandmothers and others waved their handkerchiefs, dabbed their eyes and called out their last goodbyes.

We children, full of excitement by now, turned round in our seats and waved back until we finally turned the corner at the bottom of the road, and the coach moved off out of sight. At no time had anything been said about our final destination. The teachers were in charge of things - and that was that, as far as we were concerned.

As it turned out, the charabanc took us only a very short distance to the nearest railway station at Forest Gate, where we were slowly shepherded along the pavements, in groups, into the station entrance and down the staircase to the platform below.

Our grandfather worked on the railway at another local station (Stratford), and my brothers and I had travelled a few stops up and down the line on the steam trains with him as an occasional treat. Furthermore, our great-grandmother lived in a house overlooking Forest Gate Station, and we were used to paying her fairly regular visits. Therefore our departure point from East London was familiar to us. When we left, on that hot and sunny Friday morning, there was nothing to be seen of Great-Grandma. She was very old, with poor eyesight, so she could hardly have been expected to wave goodbye to us from an upstairs window. However,

I do remember that I glanced up at the house as we entered the station, just in case she was there.

By the time we had all finally boarded the train, in the combined chaotic states of real excitement and blind panic, we were already on our own, as it were, although travelling under the discipline and authority of the teaching staff and their helpers. I think we probably travelled in our classroom groups, with the teachers who taught us all of our subjects throughout the school week, and, if so, we were in the care of persons that we had come to know fairly well. I was fortunate enough to be in the same group as my elder brother, and so we travelled on the train together; but our younger brother was in a different classroom group from ours, and so we soon lost sight of him right from the start of things.

I don't know whether Mum and Dad had been told that we would all finish up together in the same place, but this certainly did not turn out to be the case. I am sure that we trusted those who were in charge of things. We just left everything up to them and enjoyed the excitement of a long train journey to a strange, and as yet unknown, destination. It was certainly a novel experience to be travelling with school friends and sharing picnic lunches en route. Children did not often have that sort of freedom at that age in those days. As it was a corridor train, it was something of a nightmare for the teachers who were trying to keep an eye on us. Children were constantly making trips to the toilet, opening the windows (and leaning out of them) on the way, and 'forgetting' to return to the safety of the seating compartment afterwards. It was interesting to wander up and down, taking note of who was sitting where, and with whom. There was at least some comfort in the knowledge that wherever we were going we were all together, and in the company of friends.

We lost count of the number of times that the train suddenly and unexpectedly roared into a tunnel, plunging everything into complete darkness, except for a small glimmer of light from the tiny 'bulkhead' fittings, with the black smoke and smuts from the engine filling the compartment through any of the windows that were left open. It was a tiring journey. As it was a very warm day, the windows were opened and closed quite a few times during the course of it. There were no official stops made on the journey, but only those at various places for signals.

By the time we arrived at our destination I was very tired, so I have only a vague recollection of us leaving the train - possibly at Ipswich - and boarding a motor coach to take us to Kesgrave, a small village (in those days) on the eastern side of Ipswich.

Upon our arrival at the village school, we were assembled in the main hall, where trestle tables and chairs had been set up. A hot meal had been prepared by women volunteers, who stood ready and waiting to serve it to us.

By the time the meal was finally over, we noticed that a number of other people had arrived at the school. They stood quietly at the back of the hall in small groups, surveying us intently and talking softly amongst themselves in their rather strange Suffolk accents. Then the local officials, in the company of our teachers, began the task of allocating us, either singly or in pairs, to these local residents. I do not remember any particular part of that procedure at all. I can only think that my elder brother must have done most of the talking on our behalf, and I shudder to think how I would have managed if I had been on my own.

We were both duly allocated to a Mrs Tibbs, who, after a few written formalities and verbal instructions, was eventually allowed to take us from the school. We crossed the main road and walked up the unmade road opposite the school, to her semi-detached bungalow in Windrush Road. It was something of a comfort to us, as we walked along quietly with Mrs Tibbs, feeling very strange in her company, and nervous of making any replies to her questions, to see our school friends trooping off with other strangers along the same road. At least we were all in the same boat, as the saying goes! What an extraordinary day it had been! Our departure from East London, that morning, would have been just too painful to contemplate had we not, by this time, become desperately tired. Some of the younger children had 'given up' a long time ago. They were tired, dispirited, and inconsolably tearful. For our part, we tried hard to ignore the groups of local children who were gathered at their garden gateways along the road. They stared at us, and - even worse! - whispered between themselves, until we finally stumbled up the pathway to the front door of Mrs Tibbs' bungalow.

By this time it was early evening, and, once we were inside the door, all that my brother and I really wanted to do was to find somewhere we could lie down and go to sleep. We had never been away from home on our own before - apart from one or two very short weekend breaks with our grandparents or aunts and uncles - and the strain was beginning to tell. Perhaps we hoped that if we went to sleep, we might awake to find that it had all been a bad dream, that we were still back home again with all the family, and that there had been no evacuation scheme after all.

However, the next day we awoke to find ourselves still in strange surroundings. It was a Saturday, but that's just about all I can remember of it. I believe that our school teacher and the local officials called at our new abode to check that the first overnight stay had been satisfactory to all concerned. There may also have been some further talk or actions agreed, at that time, about notifying our parents as to our new address, or this might have been left until we reassembled at Kesgrave School on the following Monday morning.

We made anxious enquiries as to the whereabouts of our younger brother, Ron, and we were assured that he was OK, but, unfortunately, he had gone somewhere else with a different party from the school. Eventually, some weeks later, that place was given a name: the village of Grundisburgh. He was accommodated five miles or so as the crow flies from where we were staying, but as far as we were concerned it could have been on another planet! In the meantime, we were assured that our parents would definitely know where he was. We just had to accept the fact and trust the teachers.

Everyone around us seemed to be in a very anxious and preoccupied state about everything anyway. Above all, there was news of grim developments in the European crisis. The next day, that fateful Sunday, 3 September, at 11 a.m., people gathered around their radios to hear the latest news bulletin from London. The chimes of Big Ben sounded and then, after a rather ominous pause, the prime minister, Neville Chamberlain, announced in a very grave tone of voice that the final ultimatums made to the German Government had been rejected, and therefore, without any further reassurances from the latter, His Majesty's Government had no other course but to consider itself to be at war with Nazi Germany.

There were some grim faces gathered around the radio in the bungalow where we were staying. Mrs Tibbs' teenage son, Billy, cried out, "I told you so!"

That was it, then - we were finally at war.

During the few hours that we had been living in Kesgrave, my brother and I had discovered that immediately behind the property, to the south, there was a vast expanse of open heathland. This was Martlesham Heath, at the eastern end of which were the runways, and all the hangars and ancillary buildings, of a large civilian aerodrome - Martlesham.

Very shortly after the radio broadcast, we all went out into the road to watch a constant stream of brightly coloured aircraft - red, blue, silver and yellow - taking off. They circled round the aerodrome before heading off inland. Then another sound shattered the silence which had followed the departure of the aircraft: an air-raid siren. Things were really getting off to a flying start!

Before the all-clear sounded, all sorts of rumours passed up and down the road. It was even said by some persons who worked at the aerodrome that an enemy plane had been spotted on reconnaissance - hence the siren. Billy pointed out to us, with a touch of irony, that we seemed to have been evacuated to a site that might very soon become the target of an early bombing raid by the Germans. That was my abiding thought on the day that war finally broke out.

KESGRAVE

My detailed recollections of the next five months or so are few. Only the occasional brief flash of some colourful or emotional incident reminds me of the sadness, loneliness and great anxiety that we must have felt day by day.

The months slowly passed from autumn into the first winter of the war, and the nights grew darker and colder. Blackout curfews were introduced, and the local residents struggled to come to terms with this new and somewhat strange restriction, together with many others, which were announced almost daily on the radio.

Some of the older evacuees were severely reprimanded for trying to light fires on the nearby heathland, in the dark, in the hope, as they put it, of smoking rabbits out of their burrows.

At the local infant school the conditions in the classrooms were never anything less than chaotic. I shared a desk with a girl named Laurina Barry, from Purfleet. Purfleet sounded like a strange, exotic place to me at the time, and Laurina Barry seemed such a posh name; perhaps that's why I've remembered both of those two items.

One of my clearer schooltime memories, however, is of the playtimes. The playground led out directly on to the heath itself, and there was no boundary fence. We used to deliberately move further and further away from the school on to the heath, and when the whistle blew for our return to the classroom we pretended we'd not heard it. When someone finally arrived to escort us back, we would blame the overcrowded playground as the reason for our venturesome activities. In fact, we were attracted by the sense of freedom that the open space gave us. It was in such sharp contrast to the confined and grimy playground we'd been used to in East London.

For us evacuees, it was a time of complete and absolute disorientation. Parental authority had suddenly been removed, and foster-parents were unsure of how far they should take upon themselves the control and discipline of the newcomers, so the evacuees were generally left in limbo, to settle in as best they could.

We used to meet up in the evenings after school, and at weekends, and we once tried to smoke rolled-up newspaper! Don't ask me why! All I can add is that it never caught on - as far as my elder brother and I were concerned.

We also made ourselves bows and arrows. Was this, perhaps subconsciously, some form of juvenile self-defence, or were we just inspired by the fact that we were now living in the country? Again, I do not know. There was an old man living in a bungalow on the opposite side of our road, and we used to shoot arrows on to his roof. When he heard something of our activities, he would open his front door and come rushing down the pathway brandishing his stick and yelling at us as we ran away!

We were used to well-made, gas-lit streets and pavements where we had come from in East London, but here in our turning there was only an unmade road with raised footpaths on either side. During the winter months, the road would either become a muddy quagmire, or it would be rock hard and covered in thick ice. One would have needed a tank to be able to travel along it.

One Sunday afternoon in the early autumn, the evacuees all met up after lunch on a nearby piece of waste ground as usual. Some members of the party had been out playing on a previously unexplored part of the heath that morning, and they had discovered a door in a long, high brick wall. The door led into a large kitchen garden and orchard, at the back of a large, apparently empty house. We decided to pick some of the apples in the orchard, and we set off with that idea in mind.

By the time we arrived, the advance party had discovered that the apples themselves were bitter and not especially nice. We explored further and in no time we found our way through a conservatory and into a large dining room. The room was empty, except for the brass curtain rods and rings, which hung above the large windows. It is possible that the place was about to be taken over by the MOD for military purposes (in a matter of days or weeks). Some members of our party had brought shopping bags, and somehow the curtain rods were removed and the brass rings were bagged along with some of the apples.

We left the building, and we were making our way through the walled garden when suddenly we heard a man's voice from behind us shouting, "STOP! Where are you going with that lot?"

We turned round and saw a gamekeeper-like character, standing there with a shotgun pointing directly at us. What a panic followed! We fled through the open door, expecting at any moment to hear shots being fired at us. As we ran past a terraced area at the front of the house and down a grassy slope towards a small lake, I was overtaken by a much older, larger girl, who was scattering the contents of her shopping bag and screaming at the top of her voice as she went.

We veered off into some trees on the right-hand side of the lake, and pushed through the boundary hedge into a road which lay on the other side. I realised later that this was the old road from Kesgrave to Little Bealings.

We made our way back to the village by a

circuitous route, but we were too afraid to return to our lodgings in case the police were waiting for us there. We stayed out until after it was dark, but, to our surprise and relief, nothing was said at all – or ever. The next day at school (which we attended with some trepidation) there were no questions to face. Perhaps people had more important things on their minds at the time.

The family that we were staying with was comprised of Mrs Tibbs (there was never any mention of Mr Tibbs) and her two teenage sons, Billy and Fred, both of whom worked at a well-known firm called Ransomes, in Ipswich. Billy was only just of working age, but Fred was a bit older, and he hoped he would soon be called up for service in the Royal Navy. He talked a lot about his early training, which, if he was fortunate, would take place at HMS *Ganges* – a nearby training establishment. He showed us young boys pictures of the tall mast on the parade ground, which had to be scaled as part of the passing-out ceremony. Little did I know, at the time, that my thirty-something-year-old father – a habitual smoker with three sons – would himself be scaling that mast within the next two years, to complete his own course of training. Dad claimed, when we talked about things later on, that he had done so but we never fully believed him. However, I have been assured, only recently, that we were wrong. He would have had to scale it. So there! It's a bit late to say so now, but I'm sorry, Dad. You did better – *much* better than we gave you credit for.

My older brother and I certainly missed the company of our younger brother, Ron; but, more especially, we missed Dad.

I can clearly recall those dark, cold nights with the fire burning in the sitting-room fireplace, casting shadows across the otherwise unlit room. Only the orange glow from the waveband indicator on the wireless set reminded us that we were still in touch with the wide outside world. We were allowed to listen to a radio programme called *The Ovaltineys,* and I wonder if that must have been on a commercial station. There was a character called, I think, Uncle Mac. (Was it? I'm not sure.) The programme would start with a song, which went: "We are The Ovaltineys, little girls and boys . . ." sung by a group of children. The words of the song that was sung at the end of every programme went:

Goodnight, children everywhere.
Your daddy thinks of you tonight.
Lay your head upon your pillow;
Don't be a kid or a weeping willow.
Close your eyes and say a prayer
And surely you can find a kiss to spare.
Though daddy's far away, he's with you night and day.
Goodnight, children – EVERYWHERE!

Uncle Mac would say very solemnly, "Goodnight, children - goodnight!"

I'm sure that Mrs Tibbs loved the radio. She probably thought she was being extra kind in allowing us to listen to the children's programmes, but, even so, our sadness was still there after every programme, though we did our best not to show it.

There are other songs I recall from the radio broadcasts that I heard at that time. Judy Garland had just made a film from which the hit song was 'Somewhere over the Rainbow', and Vera Lynn had recorded 'The White Cliffs of Dover'. Whenever these songs were broadcast (which was quite often), they struck a chord in our hearts. Even today they are a very poignant reminder of our feelings in those early months of the war. Later on we heard 'We're Going to Hang out the Washing on the Siegfried Line', but this song became rather less popular when the Germans overran the Benelux countries and Western France during the following year (1940).

I think Tommy Handley was still around on the radio to cheer us up, and stars like him and George Formby also did a lot to entertain the troops and the workers in the munitions factories. We certainly all needed and appreciated their efforts to make us laugh once in a while.

I don't recall much about Mrs Tibbs - I think she was a fairly quiet but authoritative type. She gave the orders to her 'henchmen', Fred and Billy, and they carried them out. If she decided that the chicken pecking away happily in the back garden had to be killed for the Sunday lunch, she gave the word; and within minutes the poor thing was dead. There it was on the kitchen table being plucked and disembowelled while it was still warm. These were country people who had their own way of living and doing things, whereas we had been brought up in a different sort of home in East London.

In London we had had to go to church and Sunday school at least twice every Sunday, and after our Sunday lunch we had to sit on our chairs for half an hour with our eyes closed. While we sat there, Dad listened to a Mr Middleton's radio programme entitled *In Your Garden*, and had a cane resting on his lap for anyone who opened his eyes. With Dad, discipline was everything. Mum would be out in the scullery doing the washing-up - plates, cutlery, saucepans, dishes - the lot. As you can appreciate, the differences between Kesgrave and East London took a bit of getting used to. Our garden in London was about the size of a postage stamp and fully taken over by the recently installed Anderson shelter. Some garden, eh!

I don't remember Fred or Billy ever sporting any shotguns or rifles around the bungalow - they might have had friends who were gun-owners - but I'm sure that they set traps for rabbits on Playford Heath. It was a common occurrence for them to return home at weekends with a few dead rabbits, which were very soon skinned and disembowelled like the poor old chickens. I can vividly remember the scullery table on those occasions - a ghastly sight. There were carcasses, blood and innards everywhere - horrible! When the song 'Run, Rabbit, Run' was introduced in the early months of the war, the song had a personal message for me, at the age of eight years or so. After all these years, it still has! I have never knowingly eaten rabbit since that time, and I never intend to.

The village of Kesgrave in those days was little more than a stretch of ribbon development along the A12 east of Ipswich. Apart from the village school, the church and the village hall, there was The Bell Inn and one or two small shops, including the village stores, which had a bell that rang when the door opened. There was a lovely smell about the place, and it sold nearly everything, including bread, dairy products, cooked meats, tinned things, household things, dried fruits, wool, linen - the lot, right down to bundles of chopped wood and firelighters. Paraffin was available from the shed at the back of the store. It is a smell that I associate with those times. I'm sure that if Ronnie Barker's store (Arkwright's) in the BBC television series *Open All Hours* was given a smell, it would be exactly like the one which I so fondly recall from the Kesgrave village store.

It's hard to believe, but I've recently heard on

Radio Suffolk that Kesgrave is now the ninth largest town in Suffolk. I suppose that after nearly seventy years things have moved on.

Mrs Tibbs also had a daughter. She suddenly arrived at the bungalow with her husband, who was home on leave from the RAF. Their arrival meant that there was a hurried reorganisation of the sleeping arrangements to accommodate them and to allow them a little quiet time together.

On the morning after their arrival, the first thing I noticed to my surprise was that the edges of the large mirror on the dressing table were covered in about an inch of snow. The bay windows in the bedroom had been left open overnight, and there had been a heavy fall of snow which had somehow blown into the bungalow whilst we all slept. It must have been very cold indoors too.

The family had all been drinking down at The Bell Inn the night before, and Fred had been sick outside the bungalow on his return. Remarkably for a young man, he had a top set of false teeth, which had come out, and later they had been buried by the snow. He offered me a penny if I would find them during the next day - which of course I did. It was not difficult, but it was an unpleasant task. I must say, I have had more enjoyable experiences in the winter snow since then.

I don't remember any letters arriving, or any other contact with our parents, during those first few months. I suppose there must, however, have been some exchanges between them and Mrs Tibbs.

On one particular occasion, Mrs Tibbs announced to Fred and Billy that she was taking us to Ipswich after school "to see Mr Chips". She said she wouldn't be there with their tea when they arrived home from work. To my surprise, the outing turned out to be not a meeting with Mr Chips, but a visit to the local cinema to see a film (in a black-and-white screening) which was entitled *Goodbye, Mr Chips*. It starred the current film heart throb, Robert Donat. It was the story of the headmaster of a famous school. As he lay ill and dying, he looked back over all that he had achieved during his time at the school. He grew gradually older (with make-up) during the film, and when he finally died a large proportion of the audience were crying their eyes out - a most sad and depressing film. It was certainly the last sort of 'entertainment' we needed at the time! However, there must have been something to be said for it. Everyone was talking about *Goodbye, Mr Chips*, but as far as we children were concerned, I think we'd have preferred to see Charlie Chaplin or Laurel and Hardy.

As far as the war itself was concerned, I think things remained fairly quiet during those early months. There were isolated and tragic reminders that we were at war. A large passenger ship carrying women and children evacuees from Britain to

America was sunk by submarines, and the news caused widespread shock and horror.

Suddenly Christmas Day arrived, and with it came a visit from Mum and Dad - a real surprise! All I can remember of it is being taken by bus (these were running despite the fact that it was Christmas Day and wartime). We changed buses, probably at Woodbridge or Melton, and journeyed on to Grundisburgh, where we spent the day with our brother, Ron, and Mr and Mrs Dunnett (the couple that he had been billeted with).

What a lovely place and home that was! They had a dog - a spaniel, I believe. The village postman also lived at their address. Our brother, Ron, had been adopted, without a doubt, as one of the family, and he was obviously loving it. Of the postman it was said that you could always tell the hymns they'd sung at church on the Sunday because he'd be whistling or singing them on his delivery round the following day.

We had such a lovely day there, and it was a really wonderful meal. It was very different to where we were living. I don't know how Mum and Dad sorted out the bus timetables so successfully, but within a short while we were back in Kesgrave. Our parents said their goodbyes and they were off. I don't know where they spent the night, but it certainly wasn't with us. Suddenly they had come and gone again, and all we had left was a memory of that Christmas Day in Grundisburgh with Ron and the Dunnett family.

New Year (1940) seemed to dawn a bit brighter. Mrs Tibbs used to do some household-cleaning for a family who had a large house in Martlesham, and as we were on our school holiday she took us with her. During the morning we'd be allowed to play in the large garden, and then we'd go indoors for our elevenses - coffee and biscuits - which was something of a novelty for us.

There were sometimes parties in the evenings, and we'd be included in these. They were given by Mrs Tibbs' friends from The Bell Inn. They were always lively affairs; there was plenty of party food around, and the drinks flowed.

We would play silly blindfold games, such as blind man's buff and one where you entered the room blindfolded to the 'Court of Silence'. You then had to kneel on a cushion and perform an act of worship with the words "Oh wah tah nass Siam." When you bent forward into a prostrate position you would receive a whack on the behind, which was followed by much laughter from those who were watching. The final blindfold game - a 'Guess what this is?' game - involved entering the room blindfolded and having your hand guided towards a bowl rather similar in shape to a chamber pot. With your hand in the bowl of liquid you had to fish around to discover the contents therein, which generally included rolled-up skin or other unused parts of the chicken from the lunchtime meal. The liquid itself was coloured orange with Tizer or some other cordial. The whole procedure was designed so that later, when you removed the blindfold, you might think (quite wrongly) that you'd been handling the sort of contents more commonly associated with a chamber pot.

For me, the best part of all these get-togethers was the sing-song around the piano at the end of the evening. I remember singing all the old favourites from the First World War, such as 'It's a Long Way to Tipperary', 'Pack up Your Troubles', 'Goodbye, Dolly Gray', 'Take Me Back to Dear Old Blighty' and 'Mademoiselle from Armentieres', to be followed by 'Little Brown Jug', 'Roaming in the Gloaming', 'Home on the Range' and many others. As the evening wore on the songs became more and more nostalgic - such as 'There's No Place Like Home', 'There Is a Lady, Sweet and Kind' (or 'Passing By'), 'Bless This House', 'Come into the Garden, Maud', and Gracie Fields' song, 'Sally, Sally, - don't ever wander . . .'

A new one that I learnt was entitled 'Ramona'. By this time of the evening, the song was sung with such feeling and passionate expression that it stayed in my mind. A few years later, when I was in my teens, Dorothy Lamour hit the cinema screens with Bob Hope and Bing Crosby in the 'Road' series of films. She became the embodiment for me of Ramona; whenever I saw Dorothy Lamour on the cinema screen she was in my boyhood imagination Ramona in the flesh, as it were.

Bob Hope and Bing Crosby were also among my all-time cinema favourites, from that time onwards.

I don't recall our return to East London at all. Air-raid attacks on London hadn't at that time begun, and quite a few of the other evacuees had gradually drifted back home. It was sometime at the end of January, or the beginning of February - maybe even as early as my ninth birthday on 22 January - that Mum suddenly arrived and took us back to East London and our old school in Ham Park Road. Ron hung on grimly with the family at Grundisburgh, where he was treated more than ever like an adopted son. He remained in close contact with Mrs Dunnett in particular for the next forty-five years or so. She was always referred to by him as Nanny Dunnett.

Since the occupation of Poland at the end of September 1939, the build-up for another offensive had quietly been taking place. In the spring of 1940 the German forces invaded the Low Countries. They swept into Holland and Belgium, and with outflank paratroopers, troop and tank manoeuvres they completely surrounded and isolated the famous French Maginot Line, which had been thought impregnable.

The British Government realised that East Anglia

was not perhaps the safest place for evacuees to be, so a second evacuation scheme was implemented to take children from the major cities, such as London, to destinations in the west of the country. Therefore, in July 1940 my elder brother and I went with Dad to meet Mum and Ron, who had returned home by a Green Line coach. On his arrival, he was tired and tearful, and he remained so for quite a while. Within a few weeks we were all off once again on the new evacuation scheme.

PORTSCATHO

The first evacuation in September 1939 had been a real fiasco, and Mum was determined that we brothers would not become separated again. Therefore on the second evacuation, she joined the school party as a helper and accompanied us on the longer and even more exciting journey to another unknown destination, which this time turned out to be a small fishing village named Portscatho in South Cornwall.

She was there at the local school when the residents turned out to take their pick of the tired trainload of evacuees, who arrived that evening in August 1940. Fortunately the three of us were billeted all together with a retired local builder, whom we quickly learned to refer to as Grandpa Harris.

After a few days, Mum, having seen us comfortably settled in as part of a large, established household, returned to London. No doubt she was pleased and satisfied with herself. She had secured for us probably the very best accommodation in the village.

However, our good fortune was not to last for very long. Grandpa Harris was a widower with a widowed housekeeper, a Mrs Tathum (or "Tatem", as the local delivery man used to call her). She quickly took stock, as it were, of our appearance, and expressed her surprise that we did not have any Sunday-best clothes to wear. We were soon whisked off to the nearby town of Falmouth to a large department store (possibly Marks & Spencer), where we were all kitted out, probably at Grandpa Harris's expense, in identical outfits: white shirt, green tie, grey flannel trousers, white socks and plimsolls. These items became our regular Sunday uniform, which had to be worn on that day.

Sunday in the Harris household was very much a day of rest, and after the usual sumptuous roast lunch we had to retire to our bedrooms for an hour or so's quiet siesta.

On one such occasion - a hot and sunny afternoon in early September - as I lay on my bed gazing out of the window at the blue sky I saw in the distance three aeroplanes being chased by white puffs of smoke - gunfire! It was the first daylight raid on Falmouth Docks, and I realised then that we'd not managed to escape completely from the harsh reality of the war after all.

Within a few months of our arrival, Mrs Tathum was informed that the government wanted to requisition her unoccupied cottage for the war effort. After some weeks of agonising on this prospect, she decided to give up her job as housekeeper and return with us to her own property, to avoid any possible use of the premises by other persons. This was a very black day for all of us. Within a matter of a few hours we had moved from a large comfortable house to a cottage in which the facilities were little more than basic, to say the least. The property was built on the clifftop, above an old boatbuilder's shed and yard below.

The only toilet was down a public footpath, some thirty yards or so from the cottage. This was a small Elsan closet built on the side of the boat shed. It soon became my elder brother's task, when the winds and tides were right, to empty the bucket into the sea. I sometimes wonder how, on those dark nights, an eleven-year-old boy managed the task without getting swept away during the operation.

There was a cold-water supply to the cottage, and one drain led from the sink in the kitchen. I imagine that it discharged somehow into the sea. There were no other domestic services whatsoever. The cooking was done on a blackened cast-iron kitchen stove, using solid fuel (coal); paraffin lamps and candles were used for lighting.

Beyond the kitchen there was a scullery area with a window which looked directly out to sea. It was here that on Fridays our ablutions were performed in a tin bath of tepid water. The bath was set up on the wooden table so that one could see straight out of the window towards the dark and restless waves that were pounding at the sea wall somewhere below. The solitary candle would flicker most fearfully in the draught from the window. I used to peer anxiously beyond the rays of the candlelight, where through the large gaps in the floorboards I could hear rats scuttling around in the darkness of the boat shed underneath.

On a brighter note, however, the house move meant that we were now living only a few doors away from the public hall where our school was being held.

I used to hate carrying my gas mask everywhere, and so I practised holding my breath, and running between the hall and the cottage. I wanted to see if I could make it back there in the event of a gas attack.

A near neighbour of ours now was an old friend of Mrs Tathum's - Polly Hooper. She was also a widow, and she, it seemed, had done rather better in as much as she had soldiers billeted with her rather than evacuees. This became something of a sore point with Mrs Tathum. She was always going on about the ten shillings a week she received for my elder brother, and the 'paltry' eight and sixpence each that she got for my younger brother and me. This was the payment the government gave her for looking after us.

At school, our teacher, Mr Jenkins, who had been just our sports teacher in London ended up teaching us every subject in the syllabus - much, I felt, against his will. Perhaps owing to the lack of daily parental control, and the novel environment which now surrounded us, discipline in the makeshift classroom began to decline. In his exasperation, Mr Jenkins would suddenly let fly and throw things at anyone in the class who was not paying proper attention. Sometimes it would be a tennis ball, taken from his jacket pocket, but more often than not it would be a large piece of white chalk speedily and unerringly directed at the offender's head.

We were still fairly young and innocent boys, and it never occurred to us that our arrival in the village might have interrupted a long-standing relationship between Mrs Tathum and Grandpa Harris until an incident occurred one winter's afternoon. After school, we went to play on the beach, just below the cottage, and we noticed that Grandpa Harris was over on the far side, loading seaweed into his cart for use as fertiliser on his allotment. We had quite a long chat with him and made a fuss of Silver, his pony. Both of them seemed pleased to see us.

It was almost dark by the time we arrived home, and Mrs Tathum was waiting there to question our late arrival. We blurted out that we had been talking on the beach to Grandpa Harris, whereupon her eyes seemed to light up. With a new intensity she questioned us closely upon all that had been said.

Our excuse for being in late seemed to be going

so well that we added, with some extra enthusiasm, that Grandpa Harris had glanced up rather wistfully at the windows of the cottage as he talked to us. We said we thought he was missing us - and particularly Mrs Tathum's cooking. She seemed pleased by this last remark.

"Did he? Did he indeed?" she said, and then she started humming softly to herself.

That evening, she popped across the narrow street for an hour or so for a chat with Polly, and on her return she announced, "I have a treat fur 'ee all tonight: Polly's lads have all gorn and moved on, and they've left behind some Kellogg's cornflakes. She's gib'n 'em to me, and so I'm gib'n 'em to yous fur yur supper." We ate those cornflakes, which were very stale and very dry, without any milk or even water on them. As I recall, they were a treat! However, we never ever did manage to qualify for supper again, so perhaps she was pleased because of something we had said.

Some of the soldiers who were billeted in nearby houses were remnants of the British Expeditionary Force, which had escaped miraculously from France via the Dunkirk beaches only a few months earlier. Often on those grey winter mornings, when we were on our way to school, they would be assembling in the narrow cobbled streets for their morning parade and roll-call before marching off on another training exercise. I can remember those men, clad in their khaki-coloured capes, whistling or sometimes even singing quietly (to keep up their morale) as they trudged away in the rain. Their repertoire of songs was endless - all the popular items from both wars - but their favourite item was a jaunty little chorus which was sung as a link between certain nursery rhymes, which were themselves sung with innovation. They would return to their main chorus after a few bars of each nursery rhyme. The song fitted their lively marching pace exactly, and I include it here, because it probably says quite a lot about how those chaps felt at the time:

OH, when there isn't a girl abaht you do feel lonely!
For when there isn't a girl abaht you're on your owney!
Absolutely on the shelf,
Nothing to do but cuddle yourself,
When there isn't a girl abaht!

I think the chap I'd heard leading the singing must have been a Cockney!

I find myself wondering, as I write this, what sort of hellish experiences some of those young soldiers had to face once their infantry training was over; I wonder what terrible onslaughts and battles they fought their way through. Many, perhaps, were killed or injured in the process, before victory in Europe was achieved in May 1945. It is still a sobering thought, even after all this time.

It was now nearly Christmas 1940, and I had been getting a bit fed up with Mrs Tathum and her almost weekly reminders that the Sunday-best clothes had not been provided by our parents. I had been doing a part-time job as an errand boy for the local storekeeper, but, as everything was rationed by that time, there were no sweets or chocolates to be bought. I therefore decided to spend the money I had earned on some new clothes.

I went to the village post office and bought a ten-and-sixpenny postal order, which I sent home to Mum and Dad with a letter of explanation. Then at Christmas we received a parcel from Mum with a few small presents for each of us, including some items of clothing. Unfortunately, these were not up to the same standard as the clothes Mrs Tathum had bought us in Falmouth, and her remarks were so derogatory that I felt even more annoyed than ever. Well, at least I had tried! I don't think we fully understood what awful things had been happening in London, which had been bombed almost every night since that September! It's a wonder our parents even survived such an ordeal, let alone sent us presents!

By the end of the year the German Air Force had turned their attention elsewhere. They began their regular night raids on the city of Plymouth – particularly the dockyard areas. From the long corridor which linked the upstairs bedrooms of the cottage, we could look out over the bay and see the afterglow of their attacks, lighting up the sky about fifty miles away. Occasionally, the distant rumble of gunfire and exploding bombs would echo across the darkened sea towards us. Mrs Tathum's only son was in the Royal Navy - stationed at Plymouth! - and her husband, also a navy man, had died in the First World War. On those nights of the air raids, we would stand at those upstairs windows with her, watching anxiously as the terrible drama went on out there in the distance. There were times when she could be heard whispering under her breath, "Oh, Jack, Jack! Where are you tonight?" in a quiet but anxious voice.

On the beaches around the harbour now there was more evidence of the savagery of the war which was being waged. The flotsam and jetsam that came washing in on every tide left us in no doubt as to the awful destruction that was being caused to the ships at sea and their personnel. We evacuees often went out beachcombing, and one group made the gruesome discovery of the body of a Norwegian seaman. The corpse had been washed ashore among the rocks, and was covered with a great deal of debris. His body was buried later at Gerrans churchyard, which is in the next village, just up the hill, half a mile or so from Portscatho. The local Cubs and Girl Guides went and picked some wild flowers and covered his grave with early primroses.

Ron had not been all that happy since our parents had insisted that he should return to London from his first evacuation address in Suffolk in July, and he began to develop the habit of occasionally wetting the bed at nights. This upset him terribly, especially when Mrs Tathum's voice could be heard the next morning, exclaiming, "Oh, my Lo-or-d! You've swamped it agin!"

Polly Hooper's suggestion, to overcome the problem, was to tie a string of cotton reels around his waist to stop him sleeping on his back; but that didn't work. Eventually he suddenly broke the habit. Through it all, Mrs Tathum never treated him harshly over the matter. Complain? Yes, she'd do that all right, but there was never any real punishment or violence involved. I always had the feeling that, although the circumstances of her life had changed drastically in the short time we had known her, she was still a rock - a dour person, but oh, such a dependable person - a real tough Cornish lady who never let her feelings get the better of her.

With the longer days now gradually coming in, and because of the system of Double British Summer Time, which was operating, I can recall how surprised I was when I first discovered that the dawn used to break over those troubled seas, which our bedroom looked out upon, as early as three o'clock in the morning. After the night-time air raids,

I always awoke the next day with mixed feelings of curiosity and anxiety, and I would glance out of the window, wondering what stark events the new day would present to us.

Rumours of an imminent invasion by the German forces were in circulation for months and months, but nothing could equal the shock and surprise that we experienced one spring-like morning in April. Without warning, and completely out of the blue, our parents arrived in the village. There were no advance phone calls from house to house in those days. I was playing in the rock pools by the harbour when my brothers came rushing across the beach shouting, "Mum and Dad are here!" It seemed incredible! I just could not believe it!

There followed a joyful, tearful reunion, with lots of excited questions for them to answer. They both did their best to try to quieten the three of us, and I well remember them saying, "Shh! Shh! Keep your voices down! Remember, walls have ears!"

I laughed almost hysterically at that remark.

Dad looked very smart in his new matelot's uniform. He was on leave, having just completed his basic training. We already knew that Mum and Dad had been bombed out of our home in East London the previous autumn, and they had lived with our grandparents nearby, throughout the rest of the Blitz.

Now Dad, having been called up on active service himself, was most anxious to see us reunited with

Mum whilst he was away, possibly in some requisitioned property there in Cornwall. We retired to the local pub in Gerrans, where they were staying, to discuss the plans that he had in mind.

Later that day we all returned to see Mrs Tathum and tell her of the new proposals, which were to take effect from the very next day. The conversation with her ended very amicably. I think that as Dad was a newly recruited seaman she was probably thinking, 'And the best of luck to you!'

That evening we spent packing our things in a state of feverish excitement. It was all too much for one day! Our Sunday-best outfits were duly returned, and the next morning, when Mum and Dad arrived with Mr Thomas, the billeting officer, in his Bedford estate car, we said our rather strained goodbyes to Mrs Tathum.

Off we went to another unknown destination. This time it was to prove to be in half of a requisitioned, nearly dilapidated farmhouse, near Truro. It was almost uninhabitable, as we were soon to find out. It lacked even a basic water supply. It was a real disaster of a place.

Myself, Ron and Norman, with Mrs Tathum and Grandpa Harris in Portscatho, 1940.

Dad, outside The Bell Inn, Gerrans Village.

Mum.

Myself on Silver.

Mr Wilcocks, Blackie and Myself.

Mum and 'the boys', Newquay, 1942.

Myself, Norman and Ron, Newquay, 1942.

Lape Cottage, as I remember it.

LAPE COTTAGE, THREEMILESTONE

Our new home was in a village called Threemilestone, which is three miles west of Truro, in Central Cornwall.

Before we arrived, we stopped at Truro to collect the keys for the property and pick up some supplies. I think it was a Sunday morning, so our billeting officer must have made the necessary arrangements in advance. We took on board certain basic items, such as camp beds, bedding, wax candles, cooking utensils, crockery, a teapot and a kettle. All of these items were either new or nearly new, which made the whole exercise seem even more exciting - at that stage. There were also a number of forms to be completed by Mum and Dad, and a few emergency rations were procured to tide us over for the next few days or so. By that time we would be able to use our ration books in the local village shops.

With all of these formalities completed, we set off once again for Threemilestone. We left the A390 just before reaching the village itself (as we discovered later), and drove a good mile or so down a series of narrow country lanes until we finally pulled up outside a very old, deserted farmhouse. We had arrived at Lape Cottage!

We were accustomed to the bustle of living in London, but even in comparison with Portscatho our new home was isolated. There was a strange feeling of utter remoteness about the place. There were, however, two small bungalows in the lane, 150 yards or so in both directions (that is, one on either side of Lape Cottage). Their occupants were fairly old, retired people. We were, eventually, to become acquainted with them, but there was no one there to greet us, or to offer us any help or advice, when we first arrived on that Sunday afternoon in April 1941.

Our new abode looked, as indeed it was, both desolate and neglected, as though the previous occupants had long since gone. The thatched roof sagged, and the house was surrounded by a jungle of weeds where once had been a thriving flower garden and kitchen garden. One could almost sense a feeling of resentment from the old place. It seemed to be just sitting there, resigned to its own solitude, reluctant to accept the disturbance or intrusion which our sudden unwarranted arrival had created.

The white-painted wicket gate sagged heavily on its two hinges, and as we pushed it open, across the overgrown pathway, the bottom section broke away. This was a fine start to things, but there was worse to come.

We made our way cautiously up the path to the front porch - a ramshackle affair that barely fitted over the wide front door, whereupon Mr Thomas produced a large key which he, eventually, was able to turn in the heavy lock. The door swung open to reveal a large, empty hallway; on one side a timber staircase rose from the bare flagstone floor. Through a door to the left there was a small parlour, with a few items of furniture in it - an old leather couch, a table, some chairs and a sideboard - standing on a worn, faded carpet. The heavy, overpowering smell of dampness and decay rose up all around us as we entered. It seemed to be everywhere. On the right-hand side of the hallway was a large brown-painted door, bolted from the other side, which barred our progress in that direction.

From a quick examination of the upstairs area, we could see that there was only one main bedroom, and that was above the parlour. Another very small room led off the landing, and further along there was another brown-painted door, also locked, which denied us access into the rest of the farmhouse. It became apparent, after a brief discussion, that we were to occupy less than half of the property. Whatever facilities existed in the other part were not for our use. It was almost unbelievable.

Mr Thomas then pointed out the facilities of the property, such as they were. Our nearest water supply was down the narrow lane, past the neighbouring bungalow, and along an even narrower cart track. A spring led into a metal pipe, set into stone in the hedge. That was it! We had running water, as you might say! The outside toilet was in an orchard adjacent to the cottage. It was an evil-smelling place, completely overgrown and full of spiders, their cobwebs, worms, intrusive vegetation and rotting wood. Someone bravely tried to remove the bucket from under the wooden seat, but it fell apart in a foul-smelling and rusty heap.

There were grim faces as the adults tried to make a rational assessment of the situation and, at the same time, answer a barrage of questions from my brothers and me.

Despite everything, we boys were undaunted by the prospect of living at Lape Cottage, even taking into account the problems that might arise once Dad returned to the navy at the end of his leave. It was agreed that there was no going back, and Mum duly accepted what was on offer. As she put it, "It will do for the time being - until perhaps something better comes along."

Nothing, of course, ever did!

Mr Thomas, having thus made a detailed assessment of the situation with us, then prepared a list of items that we were still in need of in order to survive. The most important item was a paraffin stove for our cooking, and he promised to return with one the very next day. Before he left, it was decided that we should try to light a fire and make some tea - a hot drink, as it were, to warm us all before nightfall.

We discovered the remains of a sack of coal in a dilapidated outhouse, and there was a useful cast-iron trivet fixed to the grate in the front parlour on which we could sit our new tin kettle. However, the fire proved to be almost impossible to light. The twigs that we gathered were either green or damp, so they would not burn; and the small pieces of coal, and even the coal dust, seemed to have given up any ideas of combustion long ago. I felt that Mr Thomas was beginning to regret his decision to stay and see the tea being brewed, but, as it turned out, it was just as well that he did. We eventually got some flames going from an assortment of combustible items, but, unfortunately, the room began to fill with smoke, and we staggered, choking, into the open air.

An amazing sight now greeted us: smoke from the fire was seeping out through the flaking plaster on the side walls of the chimney breast, and from under the eaves of the thatched roof itself - from everywhere, in fact, except the chimney pot.

Mr Thomas took one look at the situation and then said in a tense voice, "Put the fire out or the roof will catch alight!"

There was a mad dash back inside again, and the fire was doused with water - too much water, in fact. Now clouds of hissing steam rose up to replace the smoke.

Then, whilst the adults kept a watchful eye on things, we boys were quickly despatched down the lane to replenish the water supply just in case things really got out of hand. We ran off, with the buckets clanking noisily in the quietness of the evening. For sheer excitement our new abode was exceeding all our expectations.

One other basic 'mistake' occurred during the panic caused by the smoke-out. Someone rushed upstairs and forced open all the upstairs windows; and their frames, like nearly everything else in the cottage, were so damp and rotten that we were never able to close any of them properly again, throughout the whole of the time that we were living there.

The smoke and flames from the fire had completely blackened our shiny new kettle, which was still sitting there on the trivet in the fireplace; then, having by now resigned ourselves to a mouthful of warm water to wash down some dry bread and cheese, we all settled down for the night on some camp beds which were hastily assembled in the upstairs bedroom.

The next day, Mr Thomas returned with most of the other essential items; but I think it was quite a while before we actually took delivery of the oil lamps and the stove, so what we lived on during that time I do not know.

Meanwhile, we had been busy digging a pit at

the side of the cottage for all of our waste water, from cooking or washing, which had to be carried out there for its disposal. We cleared a proper pathway to the outside toilet, and then attacked the inside of the place, rather noisily, with the help of a long-handled broom held at arm's length.

We never ever did discover what other domestic facilities, if any, lay beyond those bolted doors in the other half of the building - a bathroom, perhaps, and some sort of kitchen, maybe with a sink, and even a tap, and the luxury of running water!

For our part, the entrance hall became the kitchen, and the bathroom was little more than a basin in the corner under the staircase. We ate our meals in the adjoining parlour, and slept in the upstairs bedrooms, or on the landing - there was nowhere else.

At least those permanently opened windows helped to cool the upstairs rooms. After a hot summer's day, the heat under that thatched roof would become almost stifling, and I would lie there on so many nights unable to sleep, thinking about the events of the day. My most fearsome thought of all was the possibility that German paratroopers might be landing silently, there and then, in the field behind the farmhouse whilst we slept. I would strain my ears, nervously, and try to explain away every night-time sound, until I drifted off into an uneasy sleep.

Looking back down the years, I find in myself a new sense of admiration for the energy and enthusiasm my parents displayed in getting to grips with the situation at Lape Cottage. They were in their early thirties then, and, having just survived the London Blitz, they were no doubt just thankful to be in the peace and quiet of the Cornish countryside, together as a family - at least for a few days.

The war was well into its third year by this time, but under the leadership of Sir Winston Churchill, and inspired by his spirited radio broadcasts, people throughout the country were doing their utmost to assist in the war effort. Despite all the restrictions, and the nightly bombing raids on many cities, the buses and trains were running, the postal and telephone services were operating, and the BBC was still making regular daily broadcasts. There was a phone box at Sticklers Corner, on the A390, a mile or so through the lanes from where we lived, and my father went there to make the necessary travel arrangements to get back to his naval base. All too soon, that sad day arrived.

In the early evening we all set out for the main road, where Dad was to catch a bus to Truro Railway Station. We said our rather tearful "Goodbyes" and "Take care, Dad!" long before the bus arrived; and he replied, in the way he always did, "You take care of yourselves. Take care of Mum and take care of each other!"

When the bus arrived (there was no one else waiting for it), we kissed him rather hurriedly goodbye and he jumped aboard. The conductor rang the bell, and Dad stood there on the platform, waving to us as the bus slowly gathered speed. We waved back until he was out of sight. It was an awful feeling. He was gone - so suddenly - back to the war.

Mum was very sad as we returned, quietly, to the cottage. We asked, of course, where Dad was going back to, but this only made matters worse.

She cried, and said, "I don't know."

I don't suppose she would have told us, anyway, had she known. Such matters were top secret in those days.

Before long, day-to-day matters (like surviving on our own!) took hold of us, and began to occupy our minds during the daylight hours.

The stove was a lethal fire hazard if ever there was one. It consisted of a glass container which had to be filled with paraffin, stoppered, and then inverted so as to drip-feed on to a series of enclosed, adjustable wicks. There was no oven with it, so all our cooked food was either boiled or steamed, but we managed to survive.

The local school was some distance away, over the nearby railway track, in the village of Baldhu, and along the sides of the road between Lape Cottage and the school there were open shafts of derelict tin mines. It would have been very dangerous if we had decided to explore them on our way to or from school, so we waited until a temporary school for all of us evacuees was opened some five or six weeks after our arrival in the church hall in Green Bottom - the village next to Threemilestone.

In the meantime, we were able to have our own blitz on the house and its garden. We cleaned the inside, and cleared away the overgrown weeds that threatened to engulf the outside. Despite the fact that we were always up early, the chores kept us all busy every day until well into the afternoon.

Very early one morning, I saw a pair of foxes drinking from the spring. This was my first encounter with foxes, and I stood there for some moments watching them, fascinated. Then I inadvertently knocked one of my metal buckets, and the clanking noise sent them darting off into the undergrowth.

The hallway of the house was wallpapered, but this was badly faded and covered with large, damp, grey and yellow patches. In a very short time the heat from the paraffin stove began to dry out the paper, which then became detached from the walls, starting at the bottom. We soon had large pieces of wallpaper flapping about every time the front door was opened. Furthermore, Mum left a large tin at the bottom of the staircase to try to catch the lumps of lime plaster which fell out of the cracks in the walls each time we went upstairs, but we were not allowed to remove the wallpaper.

Our first new acquaintance was Mr Lawrence, the milkman. Within days of our arrival, he came chugging down the lane in his 1930s bullnose Morris car. The dickey seat had been converted to take two large milk churns. A turn of the tap at the base of either of these churns would send a flow of delicious, creamy milk foaming and frothing into the measuring jug - be it a pint or a quart or whatever was required. The milk was then transferred into the customer's own jug or bowl, carried indoors, and covered with a muslin cloth. There were no milk bottles, plastic cartons or fridges to be found in that part of Cornwall at that time, but we could always depend on the daily arrival of the milkman. Mr Lawrence was not a young man, by any means, but he was a fairly agile person nonetheless. He was tall and he had a wry sense of humour. He would always try to ensure that there was time for a chat. He gave long blasts on the klaxon of his car as he approached the farmhouse, so that we could be there at the gate when he arrived. He seemed to enjoy teasing us 'townies', and he provided us with an insight into nature and the ways of the countryside.

I remember him saying to me on one occasion, "Ketch 'old of that there stingin' nittle. They don' sting this 'ere month."

I did so, but I found, of course, that they still did.

I looked at him in real surprise, and he laughed heartily and said, "See – youm's learning already! They don' sting this 'ere month; they sting *you*!" Then he added, "Now, do as I tell 'ee, and git 'old of it, really firm, loike, and it won' sting 'ee. I'll show 'ee how 'tis."

I followed his example and found that what he had said was true. I've always remembered that early experience, and later on in life I knew exactly what people meant when they talked about 'grasping the nettle'.

Another person who passed our front gate was Lily. She would pass with her 'gaggle' of kids on their way to and from the village stores at Threemilestone.

She said, "Just call me Lil," and so we did. Lily had been 'bombed out' from her home in Bermondsey in London, and she must have left in such a hurry that she forgot her false teeth! She was a small, wiry little woman with dark hair and flashing eyes, and her toothless gums champed up and down the whole time that she was talking. I'm not sure which family arrived in the area first, hers or ours. It was probably her that told Mum about the open mineshafts; she lived, in another dilapidated cottage, on the other side of the railway track, towards Baldhu. She was, as she frequently put it, "bleedin' disgusted with everybody and everything". She said her kids weren't going to walk "bleedin' miles" to school every day after being "bombed aht"; and, as far as I can remember, they never ever did. I think that both she and Mum were lonely. They missed the 'closeness' of people in London. Lil would often stop for a good old jaw at our dilapidated old gate; the two of them would then stand and commiserate with each other on the state of things.

Lil told us that, when she and her family first arrived, she took up the hall carpet in her cottage to give it a really good going over, and it fell apart in her hands. "Bleedin' maggots crawled aht of it!" she said. A large cupboard in her hall was locked, so, thinking that it might contain some items that could be of help in cleaning up the cottage, she boldly broke it open. With a look of utter disgust, and with her gums working overtime, she exclaimed, "If you could have seen the muck and sh— stuff that was inside! Bleedin' old rubbish! You'd be too ashamed to even put it in your dustbin! I can't tell yer! I can't tell yer!" she repeated. "They says us Londoners is dirty; they're filthy! Mice! Rats' nests! All locked up in the bleedin' cupboard!"

Outbursts like this used to quite cheer us all up. They made us realise that perhaps our situation wasn't so bad after all. Often, after she had gone on her way, we would discuss the things which she had told us, with each of us giving our own impersonation of the poor, unhappy soul for the amusement of the others. We all agreed on one thing: we pitied the poor old billeting officer who called on her to enquire, kindly, "How are you getting on, then?"

Further on down the lane, in a bungalow overlooking the railway track, lived a retired couple, Mr and Mrs Parsons. In fact, Mrs Parsons was so far into her retirement that I don't ever remember seeing her, although she wasn't thought to be suffering with ill health, as far as I knew. Mr Parsons was up and down the lane quite a lot, keeping an eye on us all and giving help and advice to Mum on day-to-day matters. He was a rather quiet (and very capable) man, and we were lucky to have him as our nearest neighbour.

Dad wrote to us, but his letters were censored and parts were either snipped out or blackened out. However, at least we knew he'd got back safely to wherever he was posted.

Mum liked to go shopping in Threemilestone for our weekly rations, and sometimes one of us would go with her to carry back the cans of paraffin, which we always seemed to be in need of.

We never embarked on any really serious gardening, like planting seeds or anything, and so, after a few more weeks, we found ourselves with some time to spare in the afternoons.

The tools we had been supplied with for the garden clearance included an axe and a small sickle, and my eldest brother decided that we could use these to build a tree house. Having lived for months on end under the threat of an imminent German invasion, we thought a tree house would make a good lookout. My brother chose - would you believe it? - a large holly tree on the lane which led to the spring. It was almost outside Sunnycott, our neighbours' bungalow, but it had the advantage that we could climb it fairly easily. This, of course, was an important consideration. We set about the task of cutting poles and sticks of various sizes, but we soon realised the limitations of the tools which we had available. In the end, the tree house was reduced to just a timber platform, with greenery added at the sides. Then we armed ourselves with an assortment of cudgels, staves, bows and arrows and catapults and settled down to await the arrival of the enemy. We didn't, of course, expect a German panzer division to come trundling down the lane, but a few storm troopers racing by on motorcycles seemed, at the time, to be a distinct possibility!

One hot summer's afternoon, I was on lookout duty in the tree when I saw what I thought were a number of large white pyramids on the horizon. I couldn't believe my eyes at first. They were barely visible in the shimmering heat, but it was a weird and unaccustomed sight. The pyramids turned out to be the china-clay workings north of Truro, and therefore no cause for alarm (or 'wild imaginings', as Mum put it) on my part. Nobody had ever pointed them out - or perhaps even noticed that they were there - until that time.

What did eventually come trundling down the lane was another batch of evacuees from Bristol. One of them said in a rather strange accent, "Oi coom frum Bristow. Where d'you coom fro'?"

Two evacuees, a brother and sister, came to stay at Sunnycott, and they added a bit more interest to our evening skirmishes in and around the tree house. Their arrival also meant that we had a bit more company on our walk through the lanes to Green Bottom, when we all eventually went back to school.

Our tree house overlooked the approaches to the spring and Lape Cottage, and during our war games we considered the use of all sorts of alarm systems and booby traps, such as wires stretched across the lane itself; but these ideas, I'm glad to say, were never implemented. As it was, the only person that we might have ensnared was the milkman, Mr Lawrence.

Lape Cottage was part of what was originally a fairly large farmhouse, and the whole farm had originally been owned by one family. The younger members of the family had set up their own farm on the main road – a large barn-like building, which was rather inappropriately named Mount Pleasant. I think that the older members of the family remained in the farmhouse until they died or had to be moved out, whereupon the place was just left, unused and neglected, until it was requisitioned by the government. The present owners then very quickly had to vacate part of the premises for our use.

The farmhouse had two front doors, and the one which we used, on the left-hand side, was probably at one time at the 'posh' end of the place. That is, it was where the sitting room or the parlour would have been. Our front door was approached down a pathway through the flower and kitchen gardens. The other front door was on the right-hand side – on what one might call the business end of things. It was reached by means of a large five-barred gate, across a farmyard which was surrounded by a number of stables and other outbuildings. A thick hedge ran from the front of the house to the edge of the lane, so as to divide the farmyard from the garden area. The outbuildings and the fields in the vicinity of the farmhouse had been leased to another farmer, a Mr Wilcocks, a quiet, gentle sort of man who had a farm on the main road at Sticklers Corner.

I became acquainted with Mr Wilcocks as a result of an incident which occurred a few weeks before we returned, once again, to school. One morning, as I was helping my eldest brother to dig yet another pit for the disposal of the contents of the toilet bucket (a task in which he had become quite experienced by this time!), I heard the sound of an animal bellowing loudly, as though it was in some distress. I ran down through the orchard, where I found that a large brown cow had tried to climb out of the adjoining field through a gap in the stone wall. It had hoped to enjoy the longer grass, which was there in the orchard, but it had become hopelessly wedged, straddled across the wall. I don't remember now where I finally found Mr Wilcocks; he may have been working in the outbuildings next door to the farmhouse. However, once on the scene, he soon coaxed (with the aid of a big stick) the animal back into the field again. Mr Wilcocks seemed quite pleased that I had been concerned enough to raise the alarm.

He came and introduced himself to Mum, and, before he left, I agreed to keep an eye on things for him in the future. In next to no time I was helping him to drive the cows through the lanes, of an evening, up to his farmhouse for milking.

It was there that I met the only other relative that he had living with him - his daughter, Esther. She was a young woman, in her late teens or early twenties, and she shared much of the farm work, and also dealt with the housekeeping.

For the next few weeks I spent most of my time at the farm, helping with the haymaking, and other chores that came along. I thoroughly enjoyed this new experience as a farmer's boy. One of our more pleasant tasks was visiting other farmers on business, transporting livestock or perhaps animal feed of some sort or other by means of the pony and cart or the two-wheeled trap.

By this time, I had become very interested in country matters, and such things as snakes -

particularly adders. One day I was out on the cart with Mr Wilcocks when he told me a tale of the time that his pony, Silver, nearly trod on an adder in the lane as it lay basking in the sun. The pony shied in alarm, and bolted, whereupon the adder, being somewhat angry as a result of the disturbance, had then chased after the cart, intent upon causing further mischief. It was only when Mr Wilcocks managed to stop the cart and then back the wheel over the snake that the drama was concluded. For a while I thought this story was true.

Even after the time that I had started back again to school, I continued to drive the cows to the farm for milking; and sometimes Esther would come back home with me so that I could ride Silver down to the fields near our farmhouse.

Esther would say to me, "Now, then, Ken, you can pretend you're a real cowboy, just like Roy Rogers on his horse, Trigger. I guess she too had seen films about cowboys and indians and the Wild West, which were very popular at that time.

On one such occasion, when I had barely started on my homeward journey down the lane with Esther, in the gathering dusk there emerged from the hedgerow a tall, dark-haired, handsome-looking man in army uniform. He quickly fell into step with us, which surprised me a bit at first, but he turned out to be someone that Esther knew – a chap from the Royal Artillery. He was stationed at St Agnes. She introduced him to me as Bert, and I reached down from the back of Silver to shake hands with him rather awkwardly. We said our hellos, and then the three of us continued, almost in silence, until we arrived at Lape Cottage. We released the pony into the field just opposite the house, and he galloped off in grand style, just as though he too had seen some of those films about the Wild West. I left Esther and Bert, who went into the farmyard to lock up the chickens in the outbuildings for the night before they walked back up the lane together. This became our regular routine on quite a few evenings after that.

Shortly after my first meeting with Bert the school was opened up for us new arrivals in the old Wesleyan chapel down in the nearby village of Green Bottom, and my brothers and I started school there. This meant a pleasant walk of some two miles or so through the lanes from where we lived. It soon became apparent that there was a shortage of equipment, such as desks and books, and, also, there was not enough room for us all in the tiny hall. Therefore, on quite a number of hot and sunny afternoons we spent our time playing in a stream which ran through a nearby ford, while our two young female teachers from Bristol paddled, read novels or just sunbathed.

These two teachers were unlike anything that we had ever met before. They had been to the cinema a few times as well, I guess, because their hairstyles appeared to be modelled on those of two of Hollywood's female idols of those times, namely Ava Gardner and Veronica Lake. They were most certainly aware of the soldiers who passed up and down the lane from time to time, either marching in platoons or in motor vehicles, and they seemed to enjoy all the wolf whistles and other attention which they received. Sometimes the men were able to stop and have a chat, and sometimes they even passed cigarettes around. The presence of a large bunch of kids looking on at these convivial proceedings proved to be an embarrassment to all of those concerned. The soldiers would eventually, reluctantly, move on, whereupon our two teachers would get out their mirrors, combs and make-up, so as to tidy themselves up before the next lot of soldiers appeared.

It wasn't such a bad old war really, for some! I think this might be referred to rather philosophically as 'making the best of it'.

I remember one of those teachers (Ava Gardner) particularly, because she was the only teacher who ever gave me the cane in all the time that I was at school. To be caned only once was something of a feat in those days! I've always blamed that last bunch of evacuees who arrived from Bristol for what happened, because they cajoled us all into going scrumping during one lunchtime. It was a bit of a novelty; there wasn't much else to do. Anyway, we were all caught in the act by the owner, reported to the teachers, and given the cane as a result. The silly part of it is that back in the orchard at Lape Cottage the fruit trees were all laden with early fruit, and we could have helped ourselves if we had wanted to.

We all lined up to be caned. When it was my turn I dropped my hand as the teacher brought the cane down so as to soften the blow, but she was obviously used to that tactic.

She just grinned at me and said calmly, "Hold your hand steady."

I did so, whereupon she brought the cane up again, swiftly, on my knuckles. This surprise stroke proved to be almost as painful as the downward one, which she then immediately followed up with.

From that day onwards, I modified my impression of our glamour-puss teachers. They were, to my mind, what the American servicemen later on referred to as a pair of 'tough cookies'. I had no doubt about that.

Another one of my lasting memories of those times is the way in which I so often found myself surprisingly confronted with a distant view of the sea when travelling around Cornwall. This was always a great thrill, as I had previously only been used to one annual visit to the seaside for a few days.

One day I was on the top deck of a bus with Mum, going to Camborne or Redruth to buy a pair of leather boots (so that I could look the part when helping out at the farm); I looked out of the window and saw, through a fold in the distant hills, an unexpected view of the blue sea and the coastline at St Agnes. It was almost as exciting as that evening we first arrived on the Cornish peninsula, when, as the coach came up over the hill at Trewithian, we had all looked down and caught our first glimpse of the sea in the distance and the tiny fishing village of Portscatho below us. What a vivid memory that always is! How excited we all were! One thing is for sure: you're never very far from that truly beautiful coastline, wherever you are in Cornwall. It was a lovely place in which to spend those early war years. We were very fortunate indeed, and I have always said as much.

How quiet and peaceful it always seemed to be when the four of us used to walk through those country lanes on a warm summer's evening! Just down the lane from Lape Cottage, Mum noticed a robin's nest in the hedge, and on our walks she used to leave a few scraps of food there every evening for the parent birds to feed to all the noisy nestlings. This activity became something of a regular event for us, until the day arrived when we got there only to find the nest empty and no sign of the birds anywhere. It was as though they had never been there at all. I remember how surprised and sad we all were at this change to our daily routine.

One very hot summer's day, we heard noises

coming from the farmyard next door to our part of the cottage, and, on looking over the hedge, we saw a dozen or so rats playing or lazing in the sun. They must have come from the chicken sheds or other outbuildings nearby, so perhaps we wouldn't have been too happy to have had the use of that part of the cottage after all!

Before Mum was married, she used to sing with the Salvation Army Songsters at Stratford, and as we grew up she taught us quite a few of the choruses, together with the appropriate harmonies for them. I think it was then that my interest in singing first began, and it has remained with me to this day. I am particularly fascinated by any form of music or singing which is performed in close harmony.

One of the first choruses that we learned consisted of only a few lines, so it may have been an introductory part of something else - I do not know. The words were as follows:

> Sealed by Thy Spirit,
> Sealed by Thy Spirit,
> Sealed by Thy Spirit, eternally Thine.
> Thus would I be to Thy service devoted,
> Sealed by Thy Spirit, eternally Thine.

My younger brother, in particular, had difficulties with the notes or the words that we sang, so he would improvise, to the real amusement of the rest of us. He turned the whole thing into a bit of a lark. Despite our fun, Mum believed quite firmly in the things she sang about in those hymns, and they were a real comfort to her - despite our efforts!

As I have said earlier, by this time the nightly bombing raids on London had been diverted to other towns and cities throughout the country, and so it wasn't long before Mum's parents took advantage of the respite to come and spend a well-earned holiday with us. They left their home in East London, which was half full with the 'remains' of the contents of our own bombed-out home, and, as Grandad worked on the railway, he and Nan travelled as privileged ticket holders. This meant that they paid very little, if anything at all, of the cost of the journey.

Grandad had a marvellous bone-handled penknife, which he would use for all manner of things, from peeling an apple to cutting his corns and toenails. He had been born in Suffolk, and in his later years he was still very much a countryman at heart. On hot, sunny days we used to sit on the banks of the stream which wound its way through the meadows on the far side of the railway track, paddling our feet and looking for fish in the cool running water. Grandad would whittle a stick or make a whistle by sliding the bark off the branch of a bush, carving out the centre section, and replacing the bark. A number of these whistles could be combined to make a set of pitch pipes. It was all very impressive stuff to us boys. I imagine that Grandad must have been thankful to have escaped from the air raids for a while, and to be able to enjoy the company of his three grandsons for a few summer days in such tranquil surroundings.

One Sunday morning during their stay I went with Nan and Grandad to the church service at the Wesleyan chapel up at Baldhu. They were both prominent members of the Salvation Army in Stratford, and they would have been lost without some place of worship to attend on the Sabbath. It was only a small building, and there was only a handful of people there, but I remember it being a powerful service nonetheless. Maybe this was because I was in the company of such devout grandparents. At one stage, the sunshine burst through an east-facing window and illuminated the gilded lettering on the wooden screen behind the pulpit. I read the words 'Lo, I am with you always', and those words comforted me in a rather special sort of way.

One night, shortly after Nan and Grandad had returned to London, Mum woke us up with the news that something had happened. The first thing we noticed was that quite a lot of the plastered ceiling above us had fallen on to our beds and the floor around us. Soon after, there came the sound of motor vehicles being driven up and down the lane, and this was followed shortly afterwards by the sound of voices and someone knocking on the front door. We opened the door slowly and rather nervously, but it was only Mr Parsons, who had come to see if we were all right. He told us that a German plane had tried to bomb the nearby railway line, but had missed the target. The bombs had fallen into the fields on the other side of the bridge, injuring some cattle, but no other damage had been caused.

The next day was a Sunday, and we spent the earlier part of it clearing up the mess which had been caused (mainly from the ceilings). There were no windows broken, or any other obvious signs of damage to the cottage. The ceilings appeared to have more than one layer of plaster on them anyway, so we had been lucky. Outside in the lane the locals were gathering, all full of curiosity to see the bomb site itself. We'd never seen so many people out there before. It was reported that a German aircraft had been turned back during a raid on Bristol, and the pilot had decided to unload his bombs on an alternative target before returning to base. I don't know how much truth there was in that report, but it certainly revived all the fears I'd had regarding the closeness of the enemy.

We weren't, of course, allowed anywhere near the bomb site itself. The army and the civil-defence personnel had the area roped off for weeks after the incident, so we were never able to recover any fragments of metal as souvenirs of what had happened.

The nearby railway line was, in fact, the main line from London (Paddington) to Penzance, and, at about 5.30 p.m. each day, the Cornish Riviera Express came speeding down the track on the final stages of its journey. I was a bit of a trainspotter in those days, and so on most evenings I'd go down to the bridge to await the arrival of the train. How exciting it was when the first plume of white smoke finally appeared in the distance! The roar of the engine grew louder as the mighty machine surged up the incline towards me, and within seconds I would be engulfed in a cloud of warm, wet steam. The noise was almost deafening as the express thundered under the bridge. Then the engine would be throttled back, and the train would glide swiftly away down the track towards the next railway junction at Chacewater. As the train passed, I used to lean over the brick parapet of the bridge, peering through clouds of smoke and steam at the moving carriages below me. The train was nearly always full - one might say it was almost *bursting* with people. Most of the passengers were service personnel, in all manner of different uniforms and general attire, and I could see them lounging in the corridors, huddled together in groups, playing cards, smoking, or just staring out of the window as they went rattling by. For those few seconds, I would find myself caught up momentarily in the excitement of their world, and I would wonder where they were all going to or coming from.

Of course, the most important questions on everyone's mind in those days were 'How is the war really going?' and 'Are we winning it?'

The telegraph poles alongside the railway track were festooned with wires, and, once the train had gone through, only the occasional humming of the wires would mar the silence. I was told that when those wires were humming there were phone messages being relayed; so I would sometimes stand at the bridge for a while, wondering just what those phone calls were all about. Perhaps they contained secret information that was vital to the war effort!

During the hot summer weather there was a small fire on the heath, near the railway track, which may have been caused by a spark from an engine. After the bombing raid had occurred we were all a bit more concerned about maintaining the blackout, and so everyone turned out to help beat out the flames before it got dark. Eventually the local fire brigade arrived with their horse-drawn tender. The firemen, wearing uniforms with shiny brass helmets, quickly coupled up the lengths of hosepipe, and then they lined up on either side of the water tender to operate the long side arms of the appliance in an alternate pumping action. It really was a most comical and archaic performance to watch, but it was effective, and very soon the fireman had the whole area well and truly dowsed. We all returned home to bed with a great sense of relief!

Not long after this another event occurred, which was for our family even more dramatic. My younger brother became sick and he complained of bad stomach pains, but at first none of us thought he was suffering from anything serious. We all thought he'd been eating too much fruit from the garden. Therefore it was an awful shock to come home from school one day to find that he had been rushed into hospital in Truro, suffering from acute peritonitis. His appendix had burst, and he was very seriously ill.

His own recollections of the event are, naturally, rather more vivid than mine. He has since told me that Mr Wilcocks, the farmer, took Mum in the pony and cart to Chacewater to fetch the Doctor. When the Doctor arrived, he carried out a brief examination and then left in a hurry to phone for an ambulance.

Within a day or so, Dad returned (as if by magic) on compassionate leave from 'somewhere up north'. He went straight to the hospital to be with Ron, because by then we weren't sure that he was going to make it.

I remember Mr Wilcocks calling on us at the cottage soon after. He was very upset. He handed over six bars of Fry's Sandwich Chocolate. "This is from the boys at the army camp," he said to Mum in a voice full of emotion. (Perhaps he knew more about Esther's boyfriend than we previously thought.)

My eldest brother and I never did get to visit Ron in hospital; he was probably too ill to receive lots of visitors anyway, being just 'a mass of pipes and drips', as he put it, for quite a few days. There is no doubt that had it not been for the quick action of the local doctor, and the skill and dedication of the surgeon and nursing staff at the hospital, he would not have survived the experience.

Once the main crisis was over, Dad disappeared once again (almost as suddenly as he had arrived) back to the naval base; then Nan and Grandad returned for their second visit, and they helped Mum look after Ron when he came out of hospital. What a relief it was to welcome him back home again! He looked rather pale and thin, and he was obviously still far from well, but it was, nonetheless, the answer to all of our prayers. Of course, the first thing that we were curious to see was his operation scar. My elder brother, Norman, who was more grown-up than I was, could always look at such things with a clinical interest, but I was rather more squeamish and I found the idea of a really close inspection too awful to contemplate. We could all see, however, that he would have to take things very carefully for quite some time.

While Nan and Grandad were visiting, one of the hens from the farmyard next door made a nest on our side of the hedge. When she began to lay her eggs, Grandad said he felt that if the eggs eventually hatched, the chicks would not survive in their present location. Therefore he drove the hen off the nest and took the eggs. He kept on doing this until the discouraged hen went off and laid its eggs somewhere else. Then it was suggested that as a treat we should all have a boiled egg each for our breakfast, but we boys did not fancy that idea at all. Well, Grandad went ahead and boiled one up for himself. He munched away at it in front of us, and he declared it to be all right, but by then the egg and the chick had become too closely related in our minds.

Soon after this, Norman passed the eleven-plus examination, which he had sat at Portscatho, and as a result he was awarded a scholarship at Plaistow Grammar School. This school had been relocated from East London to Newquay, on the North Cornish coast about eighteen miles from where we were then living. Mum saw this as an opportunity for all of us to move on, as she put it, 'to better things'. She had had enough of Lape Cottage by this time. Norman was naturally very keen to go to the grammar school, and Ron looked as though the sea breezes might do him some good.

I was probably the only one who was upset at leaving. I knew I would miss the farm, Mr Wilcocks,

Esther and the animal friends that I had made there. However, Mr Wilcocks promised that I would be able to come back and stay with them during the school holidays (which I did!). He also said that he would look me up whenever he came over to Newquay on business (and he did just that as well). Whenever I stayed at the farm thereafter I always felt that I was treated more as a special guest than as a young farmhand.

Strangely enough, I have almost no recollections of the preparations for the move which then followed - the packing, sorting-out and tidying away of things before we left Threemilestone for Newquay. Even the form of transport that took us there escapes my memory. Were we sad as we took a last look around the old garden, locked the front door and walked down the gravelled pathway for the last time? I really don't know now. But one thing was for certain: we boys had spent an eventful few months there!

Just as we were about to leave, Esther came walking down the lane with Silver to say goodbye, and that upset me quite a lot.

Mum was right of course: Newquay was a lovely town in which to live, even in wartime, and we stayed there in a big requisitioned house, which we shared with one other family until the end of the war in May 1945.

VE DAY

I remember VE Day because it was the day that the lights came on again. I was fourteen years old at the time, and I was living in a hostel for boys at Budleigh Salterton in South Devon whilst attending the Beaufoy Technical Institute, which had been relocated there from Lambeth to escape the Blitz. The school was held in the local Territorial Army drill hall, and the hostel where we lived was one of a number of requisitioned properties taken over by the authorities in the town during the war.

Mum, Ron and Norman were living in a similar requisitioned property in Newquay. Dad was still on active service in the Royal Navy.

I can still remember the air of relief and rejoicing that there was, even in that sleepy, rather exclusive seaside resort of Budleigh Salterton on VE day.

It seemed only weeks since the town had been crawling with troops and military vehicles still stationed there. Only a few months before, a giant transporter with a Sherman tank on board had ploughed into a wayside cottage whilst negotiating a bend in the narrow lane leading down from our hostel to the town, much to the surprise and anger of the occupants, and the embarrassment of the American officer in charge of the convoy.

Now the war was over! Victory in Europe had been achieved at last! It seemed almost unbelievable that the conflict was finally over.

The celebrations began with all the local church bells ringing out joyously for most of the early morning. A musical celebration with a brass band was hastily arranged on Budleigh Salterton football pitch.

In the early evening, the sirens sounded the final all-clear to mark the commencement of the proceedings. The gas lights in the streets were lit for the first time in many years, and the blackout regulations were lifted. I went with some friends to listen to the band - our curfew having been extended that night until 11 p.m. Everyone was gathered there, including many in a wide variety of service uniforms, and some wore the distinctive light blue suits and white bandages of those who had been wounded in action. At the time, many wounded servicemen were convalescing in hotels and large houses throughout the town. Many of the people in the crowd were dancing or singing; there was an atmosphere of intense relief and happiness everywhere.

We wandered off around the town, enjoying the atmosphere. One lad observed that it was a good thing the war hadn't ended during the scrumping season, when some of them had taken advantage of the blackout to raid the gardens of the local residents for apples, pears and other fruits. Now there were lights everywhere.

We finished up, eventually, on the seafront at our unofficial den, an old smugglers' cave set in the side of the cliff, which was once used by the local fishermen for storing their nets and crab pots. We had gathered here at night during the blackout for a few laughs, the odd cigarette or two for some and for most of us some rowdy, bawdy singing, but now we realised things would never be the same again. I remember standing there looking out to sea and feeling somewhat surprised at the speed of those events which had brought an end to the hostilities. The sea was as calm as a millpond. The sun had already set, and in the eerie twilight – beyond the lines of the barbed-wire fencing and tubular-steel barricades, which stretched the length of the beach – a cluster of pink and white clouds was sinking towards the horizon. I was struck by an extraordinary sense of peacefulness, at last, it really was over.

Around the gas lights on the promenade an assortment of moths fluttered and danced, as though they too were celebrating in the unaccustomed dazzling light.

From all over the town there came the sounds of celebration: the band was still playing, car horns were sounding, fireworks were exploding, people were singing, laughing, shouting and generally letting off steam. From behind the high walled gardens of the larger houses which fronted onto the narrow promenade, there came the more civilised sounds of champagne corks popping and the chinking of glasses, became interspersed amongst the babble of conversation, occasional laughter and cigar smoke which drifted on the warm evening air.

(At the same time back at our house in Newquay). Norman had persuaded Mum to allow him to cycle up to London from Newquay with a friend, John Lee, to see the victory celebrations for themselves. This was quite an adventure for two sixteen-year-old boys on small bicycles (20-inch wheels) with no lights, few road signs, no maps, just a puncture kit and very little money; nevertheless they set off undaunted for the journey of more than 300 miles.

Luckily, they were able to cadge some lifts in lorries, and after three or four days - having spent the nights sleeping in hedgerows - they arrived in London! Just in time to participate in and thoroughly enjoy all the excitement and experiences of that unique and momentous celebration! Then they cycled across the bomb-scarred city to stay (and recuperate) with our grandparents, who had lived in their small house in East London throughout the war. Their house was unscathed, although it was only sixty yards or so from where our own house had been destroyed during the Blitz in 1940.

Sadly, Norman is no longer with us to recall his epic ride and the London celebrations in more personal detail. *N. M. Hill (1929–1989).*

I was only eight years of age when I was first evacuated at the beginning of the war, and now I was fourteen – almost a young man. There had been some grim days during that time. We had always been encouraged, even as school children, to follow the progress of the war, week by week; and, for those of us with parents on active service, there had been moments of anxiety, and in some cases deep sadness, as the tide of war had ebbed and flowed. Now, at last, Dad would be returning home from active service on HMS *Warspite*.

We had no home to go back to in London – that had been destroyed in the Blitz – but I thanked God that my family had all survived the ordeal.

I felt sure that all those good and honourable things which Winston Churchill had assured us of during those dark years of war would come to pass. The threat of Nazi oppression had been lifted. Now I looked forward with youthful optimism to the excitement and challenges of the future, in all the years ahead.

K. W. Hill *15th March 2009*

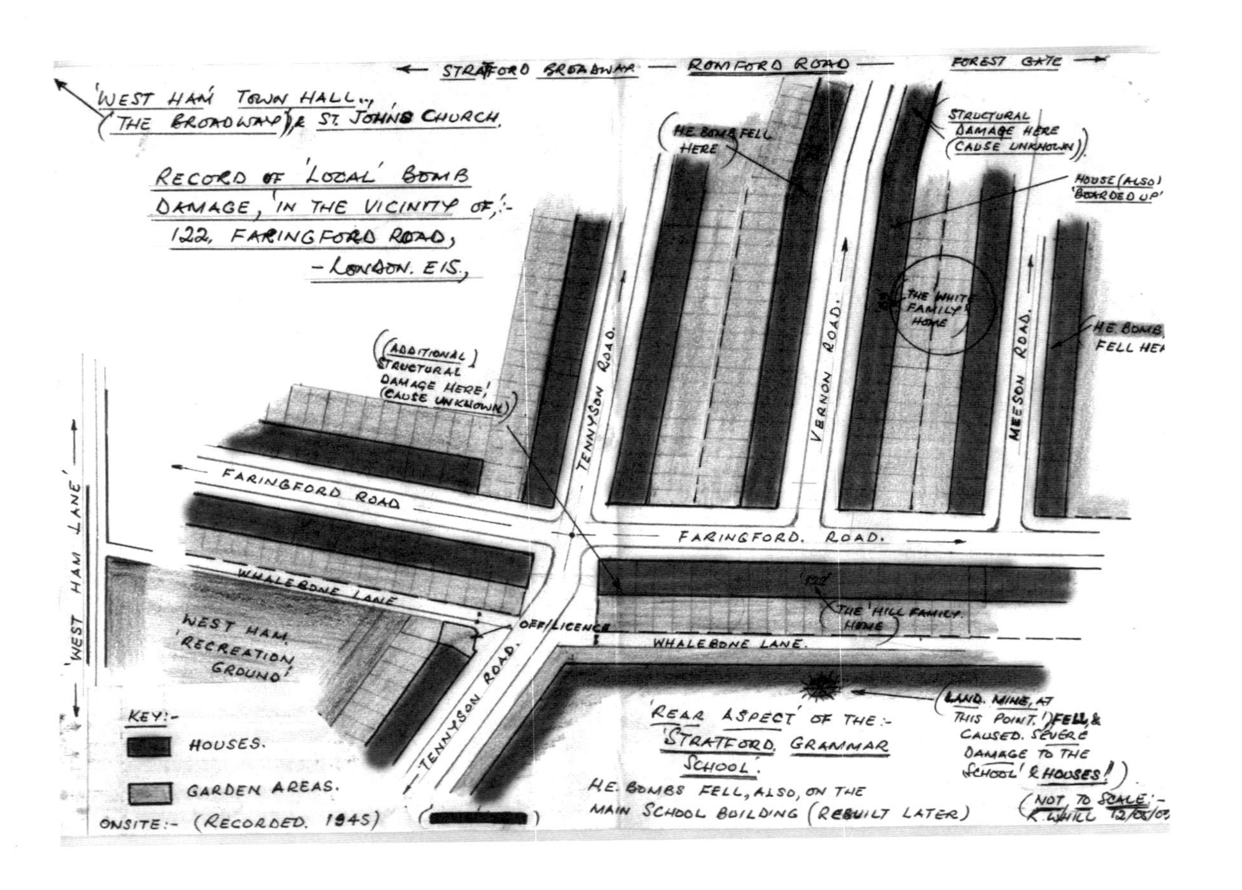
← STRATFORD BROADWAY — ROMFORD ROAD — FOREST GATE →
'WEST HAM' TOWN HALL.,
('THE BROADWAY') & ST. JOHNS CHURCH.
RECORD OF 'LOCAL' BOMB
DAMAGE, 'IN THE VICINITY OF,':-
122, FARINGFORD ROAD,
- LONDON. E15.
(HE. BOMB FELL HERE)
STRUCTURAL DAMAGE HERE (CAUSE UNKNOWN)
HOUSE (ALSO) 'BOARDED UP'
THE 'WHITE' FAMILY'S HOME
HE. BOMB, FELL HE
((ADDITIONAL) STRUCTURAL DAMAGE HERE! (CAUSE UNKNOWN))
TENNYSON ROAD.
VERNON ROAD.
MEESON ROAD.
FARINGFORD ROAD
FARINGFORD. ROAD.
WHALEBONE LANE
WHALEBONE LANE.
'122'
THE 'HILL FAMILY' HOME
OFF/LICENCE
'WEST HAM LANE'
WEST HAM 'RECREATION GROUND'
TENNYSON ROAD.
KEY:-
HOUSES.
GARDEN AREAS.
ONSITE:- (RECORDED. 1945)
'REAR ASPECT' OF THE:-
'STRATFORD GRAMMAR SCHOOL'.
HE. BOMBS FELL, ALSO, ON THE MAIN SCHOOL BUILDING (REBUILT LATER)
(LAND. MINE, AT THIS POINT.) FELL, & CAUSED. SEVERE DAMAGE TO THE 'SCHOOL' & HOUSES!)
(NOT TO SCALE:-
K. WHILL 12/05/03